I t was early morning in the Hundred-Acre Wood. Pooh sat at home with his honey pot enjoying a little smackerel for breakfast.

Suddenly there was a knock at the door.

Pooh ran to the door, where he found Christopher Robin!
"Hello," said Pooh. "Would you like some honey?"
"Oh, no," said Christopher Robin. "I really can't stay, Pooh.
I just wanted to ask you a favor."

Disney's
Winnie the Pooh
You Can Count on Me

Taking care of others' things

Is something we must do.

For if you break or lose a piece,

You'll feel as sad as Pooh.

Christopher Robin had pulled his wagon to Pooh's house. In the wagon sat a bright red kite, a colorful ball, and a wooden sailboat. "Why, Christopher Robin," Pooh cried, "these are your very favorite things!"

"Yes, I know," said Christopher Robin. "I'm going to Owl's house. Would you take care of them while I'm gone?"

"Of course," said Pooh. "You can count on me."

"I knew it!" said Christopher Robin. "Thank you, Pooh!"

Pooh was just finishing up breakfast when there was another knock at the window.

"Back so soon, Christopher Robin?" asked Pooh.

"No, it's me—Piglet," said Pooh's very best friend.

"It's a beautiful day, Pooh," said Piglet. "Would you like to join me and play at the stream?"

"I promised to watch Christopher Robin's things," Pooh said.

"Well," said Piglet, "perhaps you can bring them with you."

Pooh thought this was a very clever idea. So the two friends headed into the Wood, pulling the wagon behind them. They were coming around a bend when they ran into Roo.

"What is that you have?" asked Roo, pointing to the wagon.
"Christopher Robin's favorite things," explained Pooh.
"We're watching them while he's away," added Piglet.
"And we're heading for the stream. Come with us."

Soon the three friends came to a steep hill.

"I don't think we'll make it," said Pooh. "Some things might tumble out of the wagon."

"But how will we get to the stream?" asked Piglet.

"Think. Think. Think," Pooh said, stopping to sit down.

"I know!" cried Piglet. "We'll take the things out of the wagon and carry them over the hill. Then nothing will spill out."

They all agreed this was a wonderful idea. So Roo carried the
ball, Piglet took the kite, and Pooh held onto the sailboat while
pulling the wagon behind him.

As they walked up the hill, Roo kept thinking about the ball.
"I know," he said when they reached the stream. "Let's play catch!"
"But it's Christopher Robin's ball," said Pooh. "What if something
happens to it?"

"We'll be careful," answered Roo. "I promise."

"I don't know," said Pooh. Then he thought about how much he loved to play catch, too. "Well, I suppose it's all right if we're careful," he agreed.

When they got to the stream, the three friends formed a circle and threw the ball back and forth. It was great fun. And they made sure to be very careful with Christopher Robin's ball.

Soon Roo got tired of playing catch.
"Let's play with the sailboat," he suggested.
"Oh, no," said Pooh. "We couldn't possibly."
"Oh, we'll be careful," promised Roo.

Pooh looked back and forth from Piglet to Roo to the wonderful sailboat. He knew that he shouldn't, but before he could stop himself, a very loud "Just this once!" popped out of his mouth.

Piglet and Roo helped Pooh put the sailboat into the water. The boat looked so pretty, the water felt so cool, and the breeze was so nice that Pooh forgot all about his promise to watch over Christopher Robin's things.

Just as they let the sailboat go, the friends heard a familiar voice.
"Hey, Buddy Boys!" Tigger called, bouncing into the stream.
First they saw a giant SPLASH! Then they heard a loud GLUB,
GLUB, GLUB.

"Oh my," said Pooh, watching the sailboat sink.

"This is all my fault," said Roo. "Mama always told me I should take care of other people's things. But I really wanted to play with the sailboat."

"Watch this, Buddy Boys!" yelled Tigger, reaching down into the water.

He grasped onto the boat and brought it up.

Pooh stared hopelessly at the soggy, mud-covered boat with its drippy sails.

"Bother!" Pooh was sure things were as bad as they could get.

Pooh sat down with a loud PLOP!

"Something wrong, Buddy Boy?" asked Tigger.

"Christopher Robin was counting on me to watch his toys, but instead of watching them, I ruined them," groaned Pooh.

"We can fix this in a jiffy! Follow me!" Tigger cried.
Then he and his friends headed for Pooh's house, where they
tossed the toys into the bathtub and scrubbed away.
"Fantabulous!" grinned Tigger. "Just like new!"

"Except for this," said Pooh, holding up the wet kite.
"Don't worry. I have an idea," replied Roo. "Watch this!"
Roo took the kite outside to a warm, sunny spot. Soon it dried, and the water stains were gone!

When Christopher Robin returned, Pooh explained what had happened. And he said he was sorry.

"I believe I've learned my lesson," Pooh added. "I'll treat your toys just as if they were my very own. From now on, you can count on me—I promise."

A LESSON A DAY
POOH'S WAY

Taking care

of others' things

will keep them

nice and new!